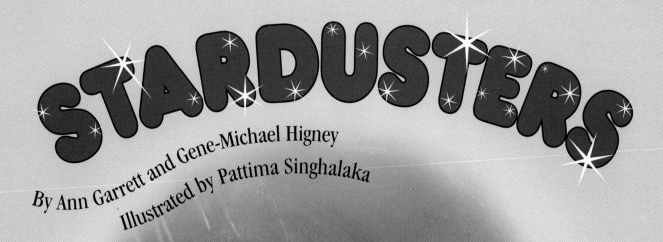

STARDUSTERS

By Ann Garrett and Gene-Michael Higney

Illustrated by Pattima Singhalaka

Moon Mountain
PUBLISHING

North Kingstown, Rhode Island

For my godchildren: Crystal Ann, Arin, Christian, Samuel, and Kenzie.
With much love, AG

For my treasured wild ones: Ayevrie, Brandin, Riyan, Christian,
and Daniel The Buckwheat Kid.
With lots of love, GMH

To Dad and Mom, for your love and caring.
To Kathy and Don, for your support.
And to my husband: your love and encouragement are like
endless fettuccini. PS

Text Copyright © 2001 Ann Garrett and Gene-Michael Higney
Illustrations Copyright © 2001 Pattima Singhalaka

First edition.

Library of Congress Cataloging-in-Publication Data

Garrett, Ann, 1953-
    Stardusters / by Ann Garrett and Gene-Michael Higney ; illustrated by Pattima Singhalaka.— 1st ed.
      p. cm.
    Summary: Two rambunctious little angels set off a chain of events that results in the first snowfall.
    ISBN 0-9677929-4-0 (hc. : alk. paper)
      [1. Angels—Fiction. 2. Snow—Fiction.] I. Higney, Gene-Michael. II. Singhalaka, Pattima, 1967- ill. III. Title.

PZ7.G18447 St 2001
[E]—dc21   2001030908

Moon Mountain Publishing
80 Peachtree Road
North Kingstown, RI 02852
www.moonmountainpub.com

The illustrations in this book were done in oil pastels, colored pencils, china marker and acrylics on Stonehenge
black paper. Title design by Alan Greco.

Printed in South Korea.

Printed on acid free paper. Reinforced binding.

10 9 8 7 6 5 4 3 2 1

The big angel streaked across the stars toward the two little angels, who were tangled up and fussing.

Arin stopped tussling with Avery and said, "Uh-oh! Let me GO! Sarge is coming!"

But the big angel got there before they could untangle themselves. Sarge looked down, earrings jingling, and said with a sigh, "Arin, take your foot out of Avery's mouth. Now, Avery? Let go of Arin's halo. Thank you."

The two rumpled little angels stuck their tongues out at each other while Sarge said, "In Heaven, we all get along!"

Avery crinkled his nose and answered, "Me and Arin don't!"

"Because you tied my WINGS together and—" Arin began.

"Now, now," Sarge interrupted, "look at the fix you're in because of all this fussing. See how dim your haloes have gotten?"

"Well, mine was real bright 'til HE came along," Avery pouted.

Arin snapped, "Mine was BRIGHTER!"

With a huge wing tip, Sarge flicked an earring as a warning. "That's why I'm putting you two on stardusting duty. Together. And you'll have to help each other's haloes get nice and bright again."

Avery blurted out, "Hey, you're just trying to trick us into getting along with each other!"

Sarge smiled. "Would *I* do a thing like THAT? Now here are your star-dusters, and there are your stardust barrels. I'll be back to check on you soon, so hop to it!" With one great wing-flap, Sarge was gone.

Avery scratched his head with his wing. "I STILL think Sarge is trying to trick us into getting along with each other."

"Well, there's no chance of THAT happening, so we may as well just get to work," Arin said. "We've got twenty-one stars to do."

"Aw, I can do twenty-one stars easy," Avery said with a snap of his fingers.

"Not if I do them FIRST!" called Arin, and he darted off toward the first star.

"Hey!" yelled Avery, rushing right after Arin.

Wings beating like hummingbirds', the two angels dashed from star to star, back and forth from stars to barrels, dusting furiously.

"I got TEN done!" called Avery.

Arin answered, "Me TOO! That last one's mine!"

"No WAY!" Avery yelled. "It's MINE!" They both raced toward the last star with an extra burst of speed.

Much too late, Arin and Avery saw they were going much too fast. Like a bowling ball hitting pins, Arin crashed into Avery, who crashed into the first stardust barrel, which crashed into the second, which crashed into the third, and so on and so on and so on.

The two angels froze, wide eyed, mouths open in alarm. A river of warm stardust showered past them, down toward Earth.

"Uh-oh!" cried Arin. "Look what you did!"

"ME?! YOU'RE the one who doesn't know how to use your brakes!"

"Never mind that! The stardust is going to hit Earth!"

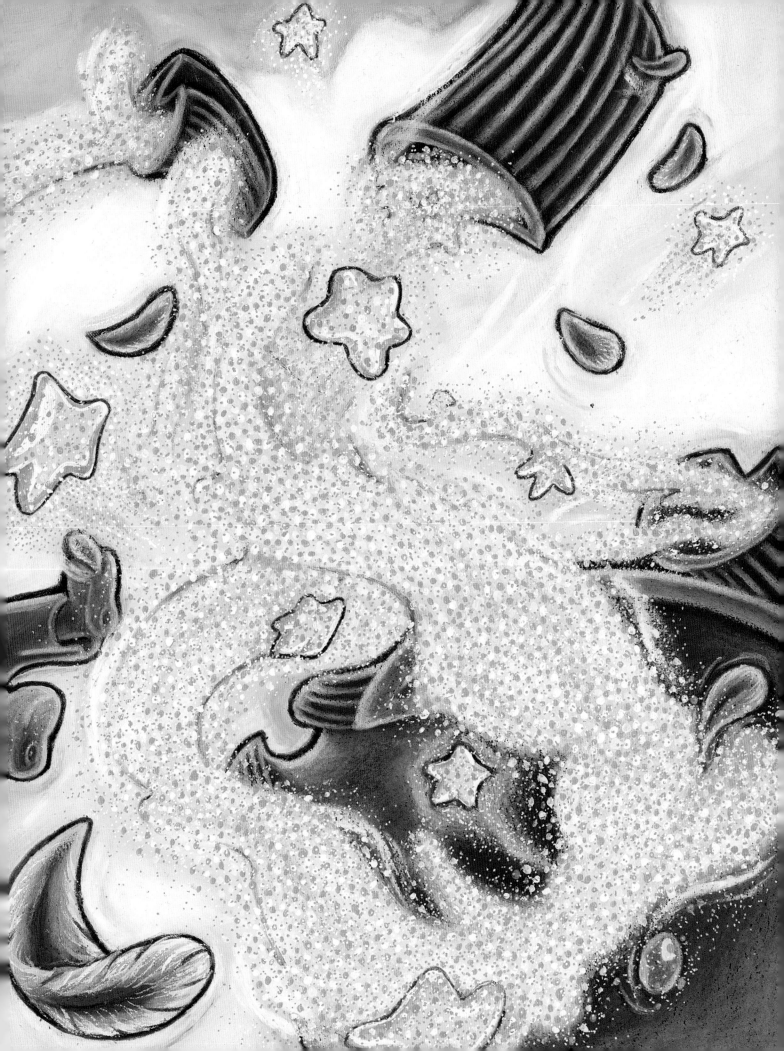

Just then, large angel-earrings clattered. "Will one of you *kindly* tell me what's going ON here?" asked Sarge, staring at the huge waterfall of stardust.

"It was ARIN'S fault, Sarge! He didn't put on his brakes and we crashed into the—"

"Okay, okay, I get the picture," said Sarge. "But now, my little stardusters, YOU have a PROBLEM. That stardust is going to hit the Earth unless you two DO something."

"US?!" cried the little angels.

Sarge nodded. "I'm not going to bail you out of THIS one! I've got to go explain your little spill to The Chief."

Arin and Avery each put a wing tip over his mouth and said, "Uh-oh."

Sarge sighed. "Report back to me when you've fixed this mess. Hop to it!" And once again, with swift wings flapping, Sarge vanished.

Arin tugged Avery's sleeve. "Come on! We've got to move fast! I've got an idea!"

"Uh-oh," answered Avery.

Avery and Arin streaked across the night sky, down, down, until they passed the falling stream of stardust.

"How are we going to STOP this?" Avery called out.

"We're NOT!" Arin yelled back. "Just fly FASTER!"

Below them, the Earth shone brighter and brighter. Above them, the stardust fell closer and closer.

"THAT'S what we need!" shouted Arin, pointing at a huge bank of fluffy clouds. The two angels screeched to a sudden stop. "We're going to move those clouds right under the stardust."

Confused, Avery asked, "What FOR?"

"Because they'll act like a giant sponge and—"

"—soak up our MESS!" Avery finished, impressed. "Good idea!"

"Thanks. Now start flapping!"

With all their might, four wings began to beat the air, fanning at the clouds.

Avery shouted excitedly, "Look, it's WORKING! They're MOVING!"

Arin pointed, "And here comes the stardust!"

At the very last second, like moving mountains of cotton candy, the clouds glided under the sparkling shower.

"Yes!" the two angels cheered, clapping hands and wings. The shimmering dust rushed into the clouds with a sound like a wave against the seashore.

"Yes!" the angels cheered again, as the stardust mingled with the cool clouds.

"NO!!" they yelled, as the stardust moved right through the clouds and kept on falling toward Earth!

Arin bolted down and under the cloud bank. He lifted up the front of his robe to form a basket. "Come on! We've got to catch as much of this stuff as we can! Hurry up and HELP me!"

Avery dropped down next to Arin, yelling, "That won't work!" He threw out his arms. "We'll never catch all of this!" The falling stuff began to pile up in his hands. He noticed something strange. The once warm stardust now chilled his fingers. "Hey! This stuff is freezing cold!"

They looked up into the clouds and felt a light coolness pattering on their faces. Arin let go of his robe and held out his cupped hand. The something piled up there too. "Uh-oh," he said. "What have we done?"

"What do you mean 'WE'?! YOU'RE the one who—ULP!"
Lightning quick, Arin threw his handful of chilly stuff and
thwacked Avery right in the face with it.

"Oh YEAH?!" Avery instantly threw some of the stuff at Arin.
And missed. As Arin giggled and Avery started wiping the something
from his face, both angels heard a *splat*...and the jingling of earrings.

The two little angels scooted to Sarge's side and started to wipe the big angel's face with their wing tips. "Gee, Sarge, we're sorry!" said Avery.

"What do you mean 'we'? YOU threw the—" Arin stopped. "I don't even know what to call it!"

Sarge bellowed, "You whopped me in the face with this cold stuff and you don't even know what it is?"

Avery shrugged. "Well, I was aiming at Arin, and—"

"Never mind that now," Sarge interrupted. "Look!"

The three angels gazed downward as the something new was caught up in the Earth's winds. It blew into countless flakes, and scattered in a thousand different directions. It softly floated all the way to the ground, and formed cottony piles everywhere it landed. It lined the tree branches like icing on a cake.

This time, Arin, Avery, AND Sarge all said, "Uh-oh!"

Sarge scooped up the little angels and tucked one under each arm. The big angel's huge wings rocketed the three of them toward Earth as though they had been shot out of a cannon.

In a moment they were hovering inches above the newly white treetops.

Avery asked, "How are we going to clean up this mess?"

"What do you mean 'mess'?" said Arin. "I think it's kind of...pretty!"

"Look, Sarge!" Avery gasped, tugging at Sarge's earring. "There's some human children! Quick! HIDE us!"

"Don't worry, they can't see or hear us," Sarge answered. "Now let go of my earring."

The children down below were creeping curiously from their homes. They began to wander up and down the piles of white, leaving trails of footprints in the "something new."

"Look!" said one of the children. "I can see where you walked!"

"Touch it!" another said.

"It's COLD!"

All at once the children began to pick it up, pat it, and toss it in the air. One brave child gathered a handful, brought it up to her nose, and sniffed.

"Oh, FROGfeet!" yelped Avery. "She's going to EAT it!"

"Nooo," Sarge said nervously, "she wouldn't do *that*."

But she did. The brave girl took a big lick of the bright white stuff and squealed, "Oooo, it's cold and makes my tongue tingle!"

In the next instant, all the children were giggling and grinning at each other with mouths full of the something.

Three angel jaws dropped in total amazement.

Arin finally spoke. "I can't believe they're eating STARdust!"

Avery answered, "Except it isn't stardust anymore."

Sarge saw a laughing boy lie down in the white powder. He swept his arms up and down, then rose and pointed. "Hey! I made an angel!"

"Hmm. Maybe this isn't the disaster we thought it was," Sarge said.

Arin looked up from under Sarge's arm. "You mean we're not in trouble?"

"We'll talk about THAT later," answered Sarge.

Avery and Arin whispered, "Uh-oh."

Grownups also gathered down below, asking one another, "What is this? Where did all THIS come from?" They began to smile, amused at their children's joyful play. Soon, the sound of grownups' and children's laughter rose above the treetops.

Sarge looked down at Arin and Avery and said quietly, "No. You're not in trouble."

Arin grinned at Avery. "Well, partner, I guess we invented something new."

Avery nodded. "But what should we call it? We can't keep calling it 'something new'!"

Arin crumpled his face in thought. "'Something New'...'Something New'...How about—'SNEW'?"

"Naah," Avery said, "I think we should call it 'Uh-oh'!"

"'Snew'!" Arin said.

"'Uh-oh'!" Avery answered.

"'SNEW'!" Arin repeated.

"'UH-OH'!" Avery insisted.

"'SNEW'!"

"'UH-OH'!"

Sarge's earrings gave a warning jingle.

Arin snapped his fingers. "I've got an idea! Let's put both of them together!"

Avery asked, "You mean...call it '*Snuh-oh*'?"

And at the same time they crowed: "*SNOW!*"

And they hugged each other.

Sarge smiled slyly as, above Arin's and Avery's proud, beaming faces, two haloes glowed brightly.

From below rose the excited cries of the playing children.

"Hey Sarge?" Arin said, "those people look so happy...if we could get permission from The Chief, do you think maybe—"

Avery finished for him, "—maybe we could do it for them again NEXT year?"

Sarge sighed, "Uh-oh."